# The BOY with BIG, BIG FEELINGS

by

**BRITNEY WINN LEE**

Illustrated by

**JACOB SOUVA**

beaming books
MINNEAPOLIS

Published in 2019 by Beaming Books, an imprint of 1517 Media. All rights reserved.
No part of this book may be reproduced without the written permission of the publisher.
Email copyright@1517.media. Printed in the USA.

25  24  23  22  21  20  19          1  2  3  4  5  6  7  8

ISBN: 978-1-5064-5450-4

Names: Lee, Britney Winn, author. | Souva, Jacob, illustrator.
Title: The boy with big, big feelings / written by Britney Winn Lee ;
    illustrated by Jacob Souva.
Description: Minneapolis, MN : Beaming Books, 2019. | Summary: "Meet a boy
    with a heart so big, his feelings glow from his cheeks, spill out of his
    eyes, and jump up and down on his chest. What good is this giant heart?"--
    Provided by publisher.
Identifiers: LCCN 2019003872 | ISBN 9781506454504 (hardcover : alk. paper)
Subjects: | CYAC: Stories in rhyme. | Emotions--Fiction. | Empathy--Fiction.
Classification: LCC PZ8.3.L49918 Boy 2019 | DDC [E]--dc23
LC record available at https://lccn.loc.gov/2019003872

VN0004589;9781506454504;JUL2019

Beaming Books
510 Marquette Avenue
Minneapolis, MN 55402
Beamingbooks.com

To Luke, with your big heart, for cultivating the big heart of our boy. Deeply, daily.

—B.W.L.

There once was a boy with feathery hair

and a heart that was bursting with feeling.

His emotions seemed bigger than everyone else's,

and sometimes they made him go reeling.

When playing outside on the yellowest days,

a loud truck might rumble on by.

And wouldn't you know it, that big heart of his

would push feelings right out of his eyes!

At night when the shadows would form on the walls

and fear would steal all of his rest,

those feelings of his made it so hard to breathe

as they jumped up and down on his chest.

But when someone he loved had a very hard day,

he'd feel he'd been over-equipped

to feel all their feelings as deeply as they,

which would quiver right out of his lip.

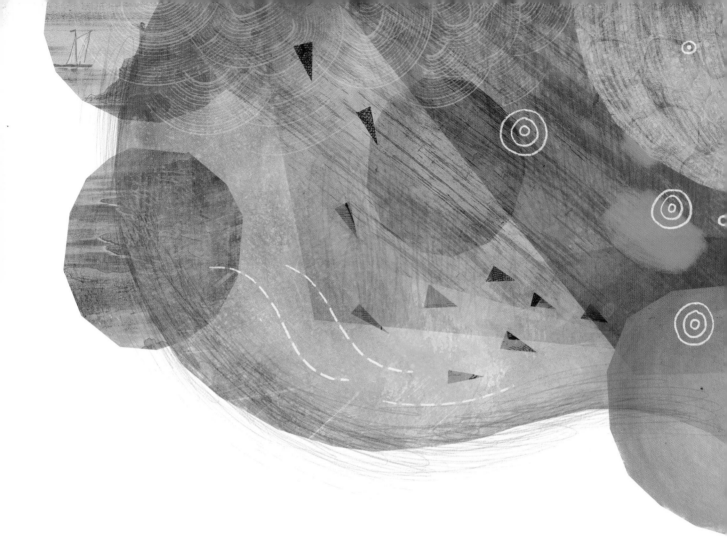

He wondered, "Why me? Why this big, giant heart

in a world that's so heavy and kind,

where all of the feelings under the sun

feel as if they were made to be mine?"

So the boy tried to stuff all his feelings deep down,

to control what he thought he should hide,

afraid that the others would make fun of him

if they saw all he felt deep inside.

Would they think he was weak? Dramatic? Afraid?

Would they call him a wimp or a baby?

If they saw the big, thumping heart in his chest,

would they not want to play with him, maybe?

But while swinging one day, feeling oh so alone,

he noticed a girl feeling blue.

He marveled: What's that? Could it be? Yes, indeed!

Her emotions were extra big, too!

"Are you okay?" the boy asked the girl.

"I'm fine. Just, sometimes I get sad."

He said, "You do? Hey, I get sad, too!

I get scared and silly and mad!"

The two became pals who shared their big hearts,

not feeling they had to pretend

when they needed to cry or to laugh big and loud,

since feelings had helped make them friends!

And soon, they noticed there were other big hearts

in the classroom, the playground, the bus,

and they smiled as they learned that it wasn't just them.

"Big emotions affect ALL of us!"

The boy and his friends slowly felt less alone

with the feelings that lived deep inside them.

Emotions might feel big and scary sometimes,

but that is no reason to hide them!

Sometimes when his play had to come to an end

or when things didn't go as he'd planned,

the feelings would run down the length of his arms

and clench when they got to his hands.

He felt happy feelings as big as the others

from tickles and hide-and-go-seek

and jokes and races and stories and songs

that made feelings glow from his cheeks.

Beautiful things would stick in his brain

and not leave him for hours and hours:

the fur of a dog, a fluffy white cloud,

his mama, a banjo, some flowers.